WHO'S MINDING THE STORE

Joe Austen

STORY STORE

CARLTON UK
Television

⊞ *sapling*

First published in 1996 by Sapling, an imprint of Boxtree
Ltd, Broadwall House, 21 Broadwall, London SE1 9PL

Photos copyright © Carlton UK Television Ltd, 1996
Text copyright © Joe Austen, 1996
All rights reserved.

The Story Store is a Yesterland/TVC production for
Carlton UK Television.

10 9 8 7 6 5 4 3 2 1

Photographs by Peter Ellmore and Simon Paul
Puppets posed by Martin Pullen
Cover designed by Tracey Cunnell
Designed by Dan Newman
Reproduction by SX Composing DTP
Printed and bound in Great Britain by Cambus Litho Ltd

ISBN: 0 7522 0174 3

A CIP catalogue entry for this book is available from the
British Library

THE STORY STORE

The Story Store is the most wonderful shop in the world.
It sells Vanishing Cream, Shrinking Powder, Move-O
Machines, Flying Umbrellas, Speed-O Powder, Tap
Dancers, Sausage Trees, Helping Hands, and an endless
variety of magical goods of every description.
George runs The Story Store with the assistance of Pip,
his best friend in all the world.
Every time the doors of The Story Store are opened,
something amazing is sure to happen...

Granny Clump was full of the joys of Spring as she made her merry way to The Story Store with her young grandson, Sammy.

But they found George in a sorry state.

"How do, Granny Clump," he said. "I'm sorry I can't raise my hat. No offence."

"My, my George," Granny said. "Whatever is the matter?"

As Sammy and Pip played with Fly Powder, George explained to Granny that he wasn't feeling well.

"Come with me, George, and I'll look after you in my garden," Granny said kindly.

"But the Magic inspector is coming at twelve noon today," George told her. "And if we fail the inspection, he could close The Story Store for good!"

"Don't worry about that, George," Granny said. "Sammy and Pip will look after The Story Store. "Won't you boys?"

"I'll believe you're better when you can raise your hat, and not before," Granny told George.

But George couldn't raisé his hat, and so he stayed in Granny's garden, helping her with her knitting as she told him all about her bunions.

In The Story Store, meanwhile, Sammy and Pip had great fun testing the Speed-O powder.

"Hee! Hee! Hee!" squeaked Sammy in a speeded-up voice. "This is great! It makes you do everything a lot faster!"

They whizzed around The Story Store, laughing and squeaking.

But they were moving so fast that they zoomed into a pile of boxes. Crash!

10

In Granny's garden, George began to doze off, as Granny droned on and on about her bunions.

When Pip and Sammy had picked themselves up from the fallen boxes, Sammy began to fiddle with the Move-O machine.

"I wonder what this does," he said. As he twiddled the lever, objects began to move around The Story Store.

They bumped into Pip, who gave a frightened squeal and ran away.

Then the moving objects closed in on Sammy, pushing him away from the Move-O machine.

Then all of the moving objects gathered in a circle around Pip and Sammy. "Oh no, Pip," Sammy shouted. "We're surrounded!"

The objects rushed towards Pip and Sammy and there was a tremendous crash.

Things were so much quieter in Granny's garden that George had fallen fast asleep. Granny tiptoed away to let him sleep in peace.

Sammy tried to use the Move-O machine to tidy up the mess in The Story Store.

"That's funny," he said. "Nothing in The Story Store seems to be moving."

But something *was* moving – in Granny's garden.

It was George. As he lay snoring, his chair moved out of Granny's garden, and travelled down the street.

Sammy was just about to kick the Move-O machine when George arrived at The Story Store.

As his chair entered The Story Store, George yawned and woke up.
"Wow! It's you, George!" Sammy gasped, when he saw George
behind him.

"Oh no!" George exclaimed. "It's almost twelve o'clock! The Magic Inspector will be here at any minute. And look at the state of The Story Store!"

As the minutes ticked away, the Magic Inspector came marching towards The Story Store.

"There's only one thing for it," George thought. "I'll try sprinkling Speed-O powder on the Move-O machine."

"Oh dear," said Granny Clump. "There goes the Magic Inspector on his way to The Story Store."

George pushed the lever on the Move-O machine.

The objects in The Story Store whizzed this way and that, desperately trying to find their proper places before the Magic Inspector arrived.

George stood in the middle of the shop, directing them to where they should go.

At the very instant the last object returned to its shelf, the Magic Inspector appeared at the door.

He was none other than George's twin brother, Alfred!

"How do, George," he said.

"How do, Alfred. Nice to see you."

Alfred inspected The Story Store, testing its various products. He even used some Vanishing Cream to make his head disappear!

When his inspection was complete, he wrote a report in his book while the others anxiously awaited his verdict.

"Well, Alfred. Have I passed?" George asked.

"No," said Alfred, "You haven't passed!"

The others gasped with shock.

"You've done much better than that," Alfred told him. "You have the best magic shop I've ever seen in my life, and you win the special prize of a gold star in your bowler hat."

There was a magical tingle, and a gold star appeared in George's hat.

"Thanks Alfred," George said. "It's what I've always wanted."
Everyone cheered.
"Hooray! Hooray!"
"You deserve it lad," said Alfred, tipping his hat as he left The Story
Store. "See you again next year. Bye Bye."
"Bye, bye Alfred. Thanks again," George replied. And George tipped
his hat.

"You did it George! You did it," Granny Clump chuckled.
"You raised your hat! Now I know that everything
really is all right at last!"

THE END